A Pony Promise

CHARMING PONIES

A Pony Promise

LOIS SZYMANSKI

HarperFestival®
A Division of HarperCollins Publishers

HarperCollins®, 🏠®, and HarperFestival®
are trademarks of HarperCollins Publishers Inc.

A Pony Promise
www.harperchildrens.com
Library of Congress catalog card number: 95-94742
Typography by Sasha Illingworth

❖

First HarperFestival edition, 2005

How and where the seed is sown, as
well as how it is nurtured, determines its final
outcome. So this book is dedicated to my
parents, Donald and Elsie Knight, for all of
their support over the years. The seed became
a tree, with branches you can lean on.

A Pony Promise

one

Tiffany Clark brushed her long red hair from her face in one short angry gesture. She stared at her older brother Tim, her blue eyes widening in shock at what he had just said.

Thirteen-year-old Tim's grin faded. He dropped the bat he was holding. "I'm sorry," he said. "I shouldn't have said that."

Tiffany let the baseball slip from her hands to the

tall grass of the lawn. "Is it true?" she asked. Her voice was no more than a whisper. "Am I really adopted?"

Tim didn't answer, but as the silence grew wider between them, Tiffany was suddenly sure that the answer was yes. *YES*. The truth rang loudly in her ears.

"I'm sorry, Tif," Tim whispered. He reached to touch her arm, but she jerked away.

"Then, you're right . . . you don't have to play with me . . . because I'm not really your sister." She mimicked his words even more harshly than he had first said them. Her nine-year-old body shook with the effort of holding back tears. Her hair fell forward again as she leaned down, wanting to hide her face.

"Tif," he said softly, and his voice cracked. This time his hand came down on her shoulder gently. "Please . . . I'm sorry. I was just so mad at you. I don't want to take you with me everywhere I go. Sometimes us guys like to play ball without a kid tagging along."

She pulled away from his hand, away from the voice and the words that stung like a whip. "Then go play with them," she said. "I'm sure Billy and Mark are waiting at the park. Don't worry. I won't come," she added stiffly.

Tiffany watched him turn to pick up the bat and the ball. He slung the bat over his shoulder and began to walk away. Then he stopped and faced her. "You won't tell Mom that I told you. Will you?" he asked.

Tiffany thought a moment, scuffing her sneaker along the concrete ridge in the sidewalk. Then she shook her head. She wouldn't know what to say to Mom anyway.

As Tiffany watched Tim head down the road toward Memorial Park the hurt settled, crushing down on her like a heavy weight. *She was ADOPTED.* It rang in her ears like a gong. She had never even suspected.

Why had she never noticed before? Tim had sandy-blonde hair and eyes just like Dad's. Mom's hair was light brown. Tiffany realized with a jolt that she was the only red haired one in the entire family. Even her aunts and uncles had fair hair.

Tiffany brushed away the tears that stung her eyes. *At least my eyes are blue*, she thought, *like the rest of the family*.

Tiffany could hear Mom humming to herself just inside the screen door. She was capping a bucket of strawberries to make jam. Soon she would look out the window and see Tiffany. She would know that Tiffany didn't go to the park with Tim.

Tiffany didn't want to face her mother yet. She just wanted to be left alone. She needed to sort out the feelings that were whirling inside so fast they were making her feel sick. Before Mom could see her she ducked through the bushes that divided their yard from the Whiley family's yard. She walked down the driveway and on down the street. She knew where she would go. She would go to the pony farm. She often crept along the honeysuckle lined fence to sneak a look at them.

As Tiffany walked, the early June heat warmed her face. She thought about the argument. Tim hadn't wanted to take her along to play ball with his friends. But Mom had told him to. Now that she thought about it, Tiffany realized that she hadn't even asked to go. Mom was always saying Tiffany needed to get out with other kids, and that Tim should be proud to have a little sister that wanted to be with him.

Tiffany thought of all the times she had wished for a friend of her own. Now, she wished for one even more. At school she sat with Melanie Colmer at lunch, but it wasn't the same as a real friend. It wasn't the kind of friendship that kept other girls on the phone giggling or lasted through the summer. If she had a real friend, Tiffany thought, she could call her now. She could confide her secret. Tiffany had never felt so alone before.

Sighing, she crossed the street and slipped through the hedgerow, walking alongside the vine-covered fence. Tiffany always felt lucky to live on

Chincoteague Island. Other kids dreamed of coming here to see Misty's family and the wild ponies. They came on their vacations. But Tiffany got to live here year round.

She reached the main pony field and pressed her face against the fence board. She clung to the wooden post, watching the ponies that grazed inside the pasture. Everything seemed so different now that she knew she wasn't really a Clark. *Who am I?* she thought, and the tears came.

Through the blur of tears she saw a pony come toward her. It was the same brown and white pinto who always came to the fence to greet her. The pony pushed her warm muzzle against Tiffany's face. Tiffany stood very still. Then, a big wet tongue slopped against her nose and down her jaw line.

It didn't matter to the pinto that Tiffany was adopted. Heck, Tiffany realized, the pony hadn't even known she was a Clark to begin with. Ponies didn't think about things like families and where they truly belonged. *And*, she thought, *they never keep secrets from each other*. Tiffany smiled at the mare, rubbing the dark brown spot right in the middle of the pony's broad white blaze.

Tiffany slipped through the fence rails and into the pasture. She had never done that before. But today was different. Today she needed the pony more than ever. She wrapped her arms around the mare's neck, feeling the warm caress of a muzzle on her shoulder. It tickled its way up her arm and whooshed a feathery breath across her neck. Tiffany inhaled, relaxing a little. The pony smelled so good. It stood still, allowing Tiffany to hold her face against its neck. Tiffany's hurt began to soften and she opened her eyes slowly, rubbing away the leftover tears.

Suddenly, the pony tensed. Her head flew up and she let out a shrill neigh, trembling from her neck, down her shoulders and into her sides.

Tiffany slid behind the mare's neck and peered out, her heart racing. Across the field a tall, thin man with gray hair was hurrying toward them with an angry look. Tiffany recognized Paul Merritt, the farm owner. He was shouting something but Tiffany couldn't understand what he was saying. She scrambled toward the fence, slipping through to the other side.

More trouble, she thought as she slid under the rough barked board. Why had she climbed through the fence? She had known it was wrong, and now, even though she couldn't understand the man's shouted words, Tiffany just knew she was in trouble.

Big trouble.

two

Tiffany watched the man sprint toward her. His thick gray hair stood up in peaks formed by the breeze and he looked mad. "Young lady!" he called. "You stay right there!"

The last thing Tiffany wanted to do was to cry again, but she could feel the tears forming and nothing she could tell herself would stop them.

He slowed to a walk as he approached her, puffing

a little with the effort of rushing across the grassy pasture. "You are not allowed in the pony field," he ordered harshly. "This is a private farm."

Tiffany leaned against the fence post even though the man was just inches away on the other side. She had lowered her head again, hiding behind her long, rust colored hair. Now she raised her chin enough that the hair slid back from her face, and nodded.

"Young lady . . ." he started again. Then his eyes swept over her and he paused. "Are you crying?"

Tiffany nodded again. There was no use in denying it.

"Well, there is certainly no reason to cry," he said, his voice softening. "I hate to see a young lady cry." He was silent a moment before he went on. "I didn't mean to yell at you . . . but a pony can hurt you if you aren't careful."

The pinto mare shoved her nose between them, rubbing her head on the fence post, acting as if she too were a part of the conversation.

That's twice today that someone has said they were

sorry to me, Tiffany thought. She reached up to rub the mare's forehead. "She won't hurt me!" she said in a voice made strong by her feeling for the mare. "I've come to see her lots of times and she knows me."

He leaned an elbow on the fence post. "I've seen you here before," he said. "You've taken a liking to my ponies, haven't you?"

She nodded again. "Especially her," she said, rubbing the mare's nose gently.

"That's Windy," he said.

What a perfect name, Tiffany thought as she watched the breeze ruffle the mare's mane. "Windy," she said out loud, and the mare pushed her nose into Tiffany's palm.

The man was studying her. Then, recognition seemed to flicker in his eyes. "Aren't you Susan Clark's little girl?"

"Yes," Tiffany said, but inside she heard her mind saying . . . *no . . . I don't know anymore.* Windy nosed Tiffany's clenched fist, rooting for attention.

"It looks as though she does know you," the man said of the pinto. "Your mother always had a way with the ponies too."

Tiffany's head came up quickly. She didn't even know her mom liked ponies.

At her look of surprise the man went on. "Your mom used to come here, like you. She was just about your size then, too." He ran a hand through his spiky hair, thoughtfully. "Well, well," he said. "Susan Clark's daughter. It's been a long time . . ." Then, "I guess any friend of Windy's is a friend of mine." Stretching his hand between the fence rails he added, "I'm Paul Merritt, but you can call me Mr. Paul. All the kids do."

"I'm Tiffany." She grasped the hand in a firm shake.

"Old Windy here is going to have a foal in a few months," Mr. Paul said.

"Wow!" Tiffany breathed deeply, rubbing Windy's nose with a whole new look of admiration. Her eyes fell to the bulging left side of the mare and she stifled a smile. And she thought the mare was just fat!

Tiffany grinned. A baby pony!

"See that pinto that looks like Windy?" Mr. Paul was pointing across the field. There was a chestnut yearling and two dark bay ponies. There were some short, fat Shetland ponies, too. And in the middle of them all was a pinto that looked like Windy. Tiffany nodded.

"That's Stormy," he said. "She is going to have a foal soon, too."

"The famous Stormy?" Tiffany asked. "Misty's foal?"

"The very same one," Mr. Paul said proudly. "Windy is her daughter. Now, they'll both be foaling soon."

"Can I come back to see the foals, too," she asked. "I mean . . . I would stay outside of the fence," she added shyly.

Mr. Paul's brow furrowed as he looked out across the meadow. "Your mom used to come and help me with the ponies when she was about your age."

Tiffany continued to stroke Windy as she waited to hear what else Mr. Paul would say.

"I could use a little help around here. Now you're a might young, but there are some things that you could help me with. The stalls always need mucking and the ponies, well," he swept an arm out at the field full of shaggy critters. "You can see they could use a little extra grooming. Would you like that?"

Tiffany grinned. "Sure," she said. "I mean, yes sir. I can do that. I'd love that!"

"Okay," he said. "I'll count on seeing you back here again."

Tiffany's grin spread wide. Nodding furiously, she said, "I'll be back."

"Well now, let's shake on the deal," he said, and he gripped her hand again. Mr. Paul nodded as if he was satisfied and turned. "I got a lot of work to tend to now. Next time you come to call on the ponies you come right in that front gate."

"I'll have to check with my mom . . . but I know it will be okay," Tiffany added.

"I'll be looking for you," Mr. Paul said, then he headed across the field. A chestnut yearling and another dark pinto tagged along behind him as he headed for the barn, but Windy stayed with Tiffany.

Tiffany leaned her head into Windy's neck. She felt the pony's mane fall across her own face and she grinned again, feeling good all over. Then the memory of her brother's news came rushing back and the mix of emotions overwhelmed her.

"I'll be back tomorrow," she told Windy. Pulling up two large handfuls of squeaking grass, she fed them to the mare, then rubbed her shaggy neck again to say goodbye.

She slipped though the honeysuckle hedges and back onto the road. The day had become intensely hot, and as she walked her sneakers popped the bubbles of tar rising in the road. *What will I say to Mom?* she wondered. *What will Tim say to me? Was Mom ever going to tell me the truth?*

Then her questions veered off in another direction. *Who was her mother? Why did she give her up? What's wrong with me*? Tiffany asked herself. The questions whirled in her head, softened by the thought of visiting Windy, pressing her face against the warm neck, touching her velvety muzzle, and breathing the sweet hay scented breath.

Tiffany sighed. Nine was just too old to find out that you're adopted. They should have told her long ago, she thought . . . unless there is a reason they kept it a secret.

Tiffany squashed a big tar bubble in the road as she walked. There had to be a reason, a real reason why they never told her. Tiffany needed to find out. But how could she find out, when she had promised Tim not to breathe a word?

three

Through the window of the back door Tiffany could see her mom still working in the kitchen, so she went in the front door quietly. She plopped herself down on the carpet in front of the television and clicked it on to drown out the hum of questions in her head.

"Is that you, Tim?" Mom called down the hallway.

"No, Mom. It's me," Tiffany answered. "Tim is still at the park."

"Okay." Mom stuck her head into the hall and peered into the living room. Her eyes filled with concern. "Is everything okay? Why are you home without Tim?"

A hard, cold lump formed in her throat and Tiffany swallowed. "I'm fine. I just want to watch television and cool off. It's hot out there."

"All right," Mom said. "I gotta get this jam in the jars while it's hot. Then you can tell me how it was at the park."

Tiffany flattened herself out on the carpet, belly down. She wanted her mom to tell her the truth about everything. She wished she would do it now. Her mom could hold her close and tell her everything would be all right . . . that she wasn't really adopted. But Tiffany knew she couldn't say a word to let her mom know that she knew. She had promised Tim.

Tiffany felt the tears spring to her eyes again.

Sounds from the television brought Tiffany's

thoughts back to the living room. She tried to concentrate on the "Loony Tunes" adventures on the screen. Through the door she could hear her mom humming a favorite hymn from church. Tiffany pushed the mute button on the remote control.

As strains of "Amazing Grace" filled her ears, Tiffany sat up and leaned into the hallway to watch her mother wipe the rims of the jars she had just filled with strawberry jam. Every now and then she smiled as she worked.

Everything she does, she does for us, Tiffany thought, and it surprised her.

Pushing the mute button to return sound to the television, she scooted back into the living room. Just watching her mom had made her feel better.

She tried to remember back as far as she could. A picture of herself at two years of age and still in a diaper came to mind. She remembered how Mom had come to scoop her up from her crib and wipe away the tears. It was a foggy memory, one she wasn't sure was even real. But she really did remember Mom holding her on the back of a large pony at the carnival when she was almost four. Dad had been trying to get her to look at him so he could snap a picture, but she had been too full of the good smell of the pony and the feel of a coarse mane in her hand to pay attention to the camera.

Tiffany went to the bookcase and pulled a photo album from the shelves. In it she found the pictures. The pony she had remembered as big was just a tiny brown ball of fuzz with four hooved legs. He had been large only when compared to her. In the picture Mom held Tiffany's waist and Tiffany held the pony's mane. She remembered she hadn't really been afraid. Mom had made her feel safe.

Turning the pages slowly, Tiffany discovered sheet after sheet of photos. There were pictures she hadn't seen in a long time. Some were of Dad on the boat, or Tim batting a ball. Some were of the whole family. Others were of Tiffany as a tiny baby, then taking her first steps, spinning like a ballerina at one of the dance recitals she had been in, or holding hands with Tim on the beach. The pictures Tiffany concentrated on the most were the ones of her with her mom and dad. She saw the look in their eyes in every picture and it was one of love. She knew a look like that could not be faked, yet somehow it still made her ache inside to look at them.

The back door slammed.

"Hey, Mom! Strawberry jelly? Ummm. Can I have some on toast while it's still warm?"

"Slow down there," Mom said. "Why did you let Tif come home alone?" she questioned. Then, before Tim could answer, "Did you two quarrel again?"

Tiffany couldn't see the kitchen, but she heard the silence. She imagined Tim looking down, wondered what he would say.

"Timothy Clark! I can tell without even hearing it that you had a fight. Can't you get along with your little sister? What was it about this time?"

The tiny knot Tiffany had carried in her stomach all morning suddenly expanded until it felt like she carried a balloon inside.

When Tim came into the living room Tiffany faced him. "Why didn't you tell her what happened?" she asked.

"I'd be in big trouble," Tim answered. "And you promised," he reminded.

"I didn't tell," she said.

"Thanks!" Tim reached over and grabbed Tiffany's hand as he spoke. His eyes were so blue, so earnest as he looked at Tiffany, that she couldn't stay angry. But she also couldn't keep the secret inside. It hurt too much.

"I have to tell," she said. "I have to know why. I have to talk to Mom and Dad."

Tim's eyes widened. "But, you promised," he said again.

"I know." Tiffany felt the unfairness of it all wrenching the lump inside of her stomach. Her eyes filled again, willing him silently to understand. "Can we tell her together?" she asked.

A long moment passed. Then, Tim nodded.

Tiffany swallowed hard as he took her hand.

Snapping off the television with her free hand, she trailed him down the hallway to the kitchen where Mom would be waiting.

four

Mom was putting the caps on jars of warm strawberry jam when Tiffany and Tim entered the kitchen. "Did you two decide to make up?" she asked.

Tiffany nodded.

Slipping the last jar of jam into the canning pot on the stove, Mom placed the lid on top and turned to face them. "Do you want to tell me about it?"

The crooked letters on Mom's apron seemed to jump out at Tiffany and she nodded again as she traced each letter with her eyes . . . M . . . O . . . M . . . .

It was Tim who spoke first. "I said something I shouldn't have," he said, the nerves making his voice crack.

"Oh?" Mom said. "Was it something that hurt your sister's feelings?"

Tiffany looked up, the tears brimming in her eyes. "Am I adopted?" she blurted out.

Shock registered on Mom's face. Then a bewildered look, replaced by one of sadness. She sank into a kitchen chair and pulled Tiffany close. Resting her head on Tiffany's shoulder, she whispered, "Oh, I wanted to tell you when the time was right." Then, "Yes. You are."

"Why didn't you tell me?"

Mom pulled Tiffany onto her lap and stroked her hair. "We weren't sure when you should know.

We just didn't know."

"But Tim knew," Tiffany accused. "You told him!"

"I didn't," Mom said. "I didn't know Tim knew."

Tim slid into a chair beside them and stared at his folded hands. "I was four years old, Mom," he said. "I knew. I still remember when Tiffany came."

Mom looked at Tim with surprise. "You do?"

"Sure! She had on that little pink dress with letters on the front. Her hair was sticking out from under a bonnet. I remember thinking, Wow, she has red hair!"

"I just didn't know," Mom repeated. "I didn't think you understood what adoption was."

"I *was* four," Tim repeated.

Mom turned to Tiffany. Pulling her close she said, "We did adopt you, but it was because we wanted a daughter so, so very much. And when I first saw you . . . just after you were born, I fell in love with you. I knew deep inside that you truly *were* my daughter. It has always been that way. I even forget that I didn't give birth to you." Mom paused. "Your birth mother couldn't care for you. She was much too young. But we needed you, and wanted you so much. We brought you home from the hospital just after you were born."

Tiffany had expected to be angry or hurt, but she felt none of that now. What she felt was loved . . . and wanted.

But Tim looked as if he were about to cry. "I didn't mean to tell Tiffany," he said softly. "Really, I didn't."

Mom reached across the table to Tim and patted his hand. "It's okay," she said. "Tiffany had to know some day."

Looking at Tiffany, her eyes searching, she said, "Do you understand that it doesn't matter who gives birth to you . . . that I am your *real* mother?" she asked.

Tiffany hugged her mom. "Yes," she said.

Later that night, lying in bed, Tiffany's thoughts raced. The kitchen talk had helped her feel better, but she still felt different. It was almost as if she were a shell now. She still lived inside of Tiffany Clark's body. But she wasn't sure who she *really* was. She felt like an outsider, looking in. How long would it be, she wondered, until she could feel like herself again?

All at once Tiffany remembered Windy and Mr. Paul's invitation for her to help him with the ponies. She sat up in bed. Downstairs she could hear her mom and dad talking over the hum of the television. She hopped out of bed and headed down the steps. Some things could not wait until morning and this was one of them.

Mom was lying on her side on the couch, covered by an afghan, watching television. Dad sat by her feet reading a book under the glow of the lamp. They looked up when she came in.

"Hi, puddin'," Dad said, using the pet name he hadn't used since she was very small. "What's up?"

She sat on the couch in front of her mom. "I forgot to tell you something today. After Tim and I argued, I walked down to the pony farm to pet the ponies." She paused, fiddling with the corner of the afghan.

"I used to go there when I was little," Mom said wistfully.

"Mr. Paul told me!" Tiffany was excited now and her voice rose. "He said you used to help him with the ponies. He asked me if I wanted to help with them too!"

Mom sat up, pulling the afghan with her as she rose. "I don't know, Tiffany. You don't know horses that well. It's not like you've been around them much. . . ."

"Dad?" Tiffany looked to her father for support. "I'm not a baby anymore!"

"I know, puddin'. But your Mom worries. It's her job to worry," he said. Then he smiled.

Tiffany didn't see the humor. "Mom!" she wailed. "You did it when you were my size. Mr. Paul said so!"

"I was raised with ponies," Mom said. "I knew how to handle them."

"Well, I can learn," Tiffany said firmly. Her chin

came up. "I'll be careful and I'll go slow. Please?"

Mom looked at Dad again. "Paul is good with kids as well as horses," she said to him, and then for a moment it was as if Tiffany wasn't even in the room, as if they were speaking without talking. Then she saw her father nod lightly.

"My favorite pony, Windy, is going to have a foal soon." Tiffany said. "I want to be there when she does."

"That is exciting," Dad said.

A thoughtful expression crossed Mom's face. "I don't know . . ." she hesitated. "What if one of the ponies hurts you?"

"I won't get hurt! I told you I will be careful. You gotta trust me."

Dad put his hand on Tiffany's knee. "I think you're old enough," he said.

"Paul does have a nice bunch of ponies," Mom said.

Tiffany jumped up and hugged her mom, and then her dad. "Then it's settled, right? I can do it?"

"Yes," Mom said. "But remember your promise.

Be careful and take it slow until you know the ponies. Each one is a little different from the next. No two ponies are the same."

"I know," Tiffany said. "I already know that Windy is the best."

Later that night, Tiffany wrestled with sleep. Prancing ponies filled her thoughts. *Maybe*, she thought, *the ponies will help me figure out who I really am.*

five

Tiffany slid her legs into the car and pulled the door shut. Mom turned the key in the ignition and the car came to life.

"I could have walked," she said.

"I want to take you the first time," Mom answered. Backing out of the driveway, her eye in the rearview mirror, she continued, "I haven't seen Paul in quite some time. It will be nice to see him and the ponies." She glanced at Tiffany and her eyes held a sparkle. "I bet I know how you feel," she said.

Tiffany adjusted her seat belt and squirmed into a comfortable position. "What do you mean?"

"I remember how good it felt to see the ponies, to be with them, and oh . . . how good they smelled!"

Tiffany grinned in surprise and felt herself relax. Her mom remembered how wonderful the smell of a horse could be. She must have loved horses just as much when she was young.

Tiffany saw the wistful look on Mom's face. "Yeah," Tiffany agreed out loud. "They smell so . . . so . . . I don't know, warm and good!"

Mom's hand came across the car, grasping her daughter's knee. "We are so much alike," she said.

Tiffany looked down at Mom's hand. Like mother, like daughter, she thought wryly. But it *was* neat, knowing that Mom could share the same feelings.

At the farm, Paul greeted Tiffany with a booming "Hello!" and a pat on the back. But he wrapped

Mom in a bear-size hug. "It's been too long, Susan," he said. Then, seeing her eyes wander toward the pasture he grinned. "You miss them too," he said, indicating the ponies. "I can see it in your face. Do you miss them more than me?" he asked jokingly.

Mom laughed. "No. But they are still special."

Tiffany saw Windy off in the distance. She was grazing near the spot where Tiffany visited, pulling up the tufts of grass by the honeysuckle covered fence. Tiffany watched her a moment, then moved into the barn, down the aisle, checking out the stalls as she went along. She had never been inside of the barn. It was long and low with at least ten stalls on each side. Outside of each stall was a pile of wet and dirty straw bedding. Some of the stalls were empty, their back doors open to the pasture beyond. Others held short, stocky Shetland-type ponies with comical, fuzzy faces, or Chincoteague ponies, tall and graceful with Arabian dish faces.

Tiffany stopped to rub a black pony's velvety nose. She heard Mom talking with Mr. Paul, laughing from time to time. Their voices blended as Tiffany wandered down the aisle.

In the last stall, a tall, blonde-haired girl worked. She mucked out little piles of wet straw and manure with a pitchfork, dumping them outside the stall door in a bigger pile.

"Hi." the girl said when she saw Tiffany. "Are you Tiffany?"

Tiffany nodded, surprised to find the girl knew her name.

"I'm Mandy," the girl said. "Mr. Paul told me you would be here today."

"Oh," Tiffany said, not sure what to say next.

"What grade are you in?" Mandy continued to pick through the stall, removing bedding as she spoke.

"Fourth."

"I'm in fifth," Mandy said. "But I live over on the mainland so I don't go to Chincoteague Elementary School."

"Oh," Tiffany said, thinking the girl looked older.

"Hey, how about grabbing some of that straw and bringing it in here," the girl said.

Tiffany looked where the girl was pointing and saw four bales of bright yellow straw piled against the wall across the aisle. The top bale was already cut open and some of the straw had been removed. Now Tiffany pulled out a big armful of the crisp bedding and carried it into the stall. Carefully she scattered the straw, pulling apart the clinging sections, covering the bare spots in the stall floor. Just as she was finishing, the girl led a tiny grey and white pony into the stall. "This is Ghost," Mandy said. "He's a Falabello Miniature horse."

Tiffany scrubbed dirt from Ghost's neck and the pony turned his face to her. He seemed to be enjoying the rub. Tiffany kicked apart a few clumps of straw and followed Mandy out of the stall, latching the door securely behind her. Just then, Mom and Mr. Paul came down the aisle.

"Looks like Mandy's already got you started," Mr. Paul said. "Well, I'll leave you to it, then."

"I'm going to go now, too," Mom said. "I'll be back in a few hours to pick you up."

"Okay, Mom," Tiffany said as Mom gave her a quick hug.

From Ghost's stall, they moved on to the next stall and then the next. As Mandy cleaned out the wet, used straw and manure, piling it in the aisle, Tiffany cut open the bales of straw with a pair of old barn shears. She pulled arm load after arm load of straw from the bale and scattered it inside each stall. As they worked the girls talked, getting to know each other. Tiffany learned that Mandy was Mr. Paul's niece. She had been helping her Uncle Paul with the ponies for over a year now, and she'd been around them her whole life.

The girls talked and shoveled, piled and scattered fresh straw. By the time the stalls were done and they were forking the used bedding into wheel barrels to push outside, Tiffany felt like she had found a friend.

six

Tiffany fell into a pattern. Three days a week she worked for Mr. Paul, cleaning stalls, dumping cans of grain into the feed boxes for each pony and lugging buckets of water, too. On those days she talked to Mandy about who would foal first, Windy or Stormy, and which ponies were their favorites. They discussed school and home, horseback riding, and what they would do when they grew up. But Tiffany never told her secret. She was afraid to tell anyone, especially her new friend. She had wanted a friend to confide in so much and now her wish had come true. But still, she couldn't tell.

The other days of the week Tiffany helped Mom in the garden or kitchen, talked on the phone with Mandy, or wandered down the road just to visit the ponies. That was when she had her time alone with Windy.

Windy was her confidant, the only one she could trust with all of her secrets, and she didn't hold back. She told Windy how it felt to be alone even when you were with your family. And how she still wasn't sure if she fit in, even though she knew Mom and Dad loved her very much, and that even Tim did too, despite all his teasing. He loved her, in his big-brother way. But she wasn't a real Clark.

Sometimes she wondered if the woman who gave birth to her had long red hair and blue eyes. Who was she and where did she live? And most of all, why didn't she keep her baby girl? And what about her dad? Questions like that crept upon Tiffany. They came to her at night when she tried to sleep. Then, in the daytime, she talked to Windy about all of it.

Windy listened like no one else. She rubbed her head against Tiffany, up and down her arm, nearly knocking Tiffany off of her feet. She snorted from time to time. She stood quite still to be scratched. But she never talked back. She never said, "Stop asking yourself those questions. You have a family and that's all that matters." She never said, "Why does it matter if you are adopted?" Or, "Be grateful for the family that you DO have." Tiffany guessed that's what people would say if she asked those questions out loud. But not Windy.

Windy just loved her, no matter what secrets she shared, no matter what questions she asked. To Tiffany, the mare's love was like a promise, a promise that things would be better.

Each day Windy grew larger and larger. Her belly was like a barrel, bulging with the unborn foal.

Stormy was growing, too. But, Stormy was an indifferent little pony . . . not as friendly as Windy. Stormy was lightly shorter than Windy, but she was a brown and white pinto, too. She was not mean, or nasty. She did not kick or bite. But she was not loving either. When it came to people, she could either take them or leave them. She had grown up in the spotlight and she took all that attention for granted.

Windy was a people pony. She loved attention, and Tiffany knew that she loved *her* too. So it was Windy she watched the closest. It was Windy she stroked and kissed. It was Windy's mane that she braided and unbraided, twisted and finger combed. It was Windy she loved and watched and waited with.

But it was Stormy who foaled first.

It happened on a hot night in early July. Tiffany was at home when the phone rang.

"Hello," Tiffany said.

"Hey, Tif?"

"Yes. Who is this?"

"It's Mandy, you goof! See if you can come down to the farm."

Tiffany could hear the excitement rising in Mandy's voice. "Why? What's going on?" Then after just a second the excitement rose in her own voice. "Did Windy have her foal?"

"No. But Stormy is foaling now. Hurry and get down here!"

"Is it born yet?"

"No. She just went down in her stall a few minutes ago. Mr. Paul said to call you . . . that you'd want to be here. He said to tell your mom to come, too."

"How long? I mean, will we get there in time to see it?"

"I don't know." Mandy's voice seemed impatient. "Look, I gotta go. I don't want to miss it. Just hurry up. Okay?"

"Yes!" Tiffany nearly shouted. "I'll be there soon." Tiffany dropped the receiver into its cradle and hurried into the living room. "Mom!" she yelled. "Mom!"

seven

By the time Mom and Tiffany arrived at the farm, Stormy had already given birth. The new foal was a brown and white pinto just like her mother, and it was a female. The filly was lying on its side in the straw, trying to lift her head to see the world around it. Mr. Paul rubbed the foal with a rag, drying the matted wet hair with each stroke. Stormy was standing at the hay rack, munching hay as if she didn't have a care in the world.

"Is she alright?" Tiffany asked. She leaned over the stall door to watch. Mom stood behind her.

Mr. Paul looked up and immediately Tiffany could see that worry etched his face. "So far she's okay," he said. "But something's not right. Stormy didn't clean her up. She hasn't even touched her."

"She barely even looked at her," Mandy added from behind them.

Tiffany spun around. "Mandy! Thanks for calling me. Did you get to see the birth?"

"Yes." Mandy said it dully, no excitement lighting her voice.

Then the full meaning of what was happening hit Tiffany. She felt her mom wrap an arm around her shoulder. "What will happen to the foal?" Mom whispered.

Mr. Paul seemed to crumble. Sitting back in the straw he stroked the tiny head. "I don't know," he answered. "Some foals respond to foal formula . . . bottle feedings. But some don't. If Stormy doesn't start paying attention to this little one soon . . ." He paused again, wiping his brow with the rag before continuing. "She may not make it," he finished.

Tiffany buried her face in her mom's sleeve and fought back the tears that threatened to appear. She looked at the filly again. The face was brown with a patch of white. Her eyes were big and liquid brown. They were lined with thick black eyelashes that brushed her face as soft as feathers when she closed them. The filly looked up at Mr. Paul once more, then layed her head in his lap and closed those big brown eyes.

"We have to help her . . ." Tiffany said.

"Let's give them some space," Mr. Paul said. "Maybe Stormy will pay attention to her daughter if they're left alone."

Something about the way Mr. Paul said it made Tiffany grab hold of her mother's hand. "Is this her first baby?" Tiffany asked.

"This is Stormy's fifth foal," Mr. Paul said. "She's never done this, though." He slipped the filly's head into the warm bedding and stood. Brushing the straw from his pants, he opened the door as Tiffany stepped back. "She's always taken care of her foals before," he said more to himself than to anyone else. "I don't know what has gotten into her."

Mr. Paul slipped through the stall door, then shut and latched it behind him. "Let's go have a soda. Maybe if they are alone for a little while . . ." His voice trailed off as he headed down the aisle. Mom patted him on the shoulder as he passed and Mandy and Tiffany fell into step behind the two adults.

They returned to the stall a half hour later. Stormy was standing at the hay rack in the opposite corner from the filly. Her head drooped into the uneaten hay as she dozed.

The filly was still on her side in the same position they had left her in. Her eyes were shut and she was as still as the night itself. Each breath barely lifted her ribs, up and down, up and down.

"Enough of this," Mr. Paul boomed in a voice so loud it made Tiffany jump and Stormy's eyes fly open. "This little filly has got to have some nourishment." He moved into the stall. Slipping his arms under the newborn he picked her up. The filly opened her eyes wide and began to scramble, waving her legs in the air, seeking contact with the ground. A moment later she was standing with help from Mr. Paul. He steadied the foal beside Stormy, guiding her nose toward the warm milk of the mare's udder.

Stormy snorted and laced her ears back. She sidestepped away from the foal and lifted a hind leg as if threatening to kick.

"No you don't!" Mr. Paul warned the mare. He laid a hand across her rump. The tone of his voice and the firm touch calmed Stormy, but it was plain to see she didn't like what was going on.

Finally, the filly found the warm milk bag and she began to suckle, weak at first and then stronger. Her mouth steadily pulled forth the nourishment she needed to live.

Mr. Paul had to remind Stormy to behave again and again. She didn't want anything to do with her foal, but she seemed to know she didn't have a choice. When the foal was full she began to play with the milk, letting it run from her mouth in rivulets, then sucking again. She looked around the room in between spells of sucking, and she seemed to take in everything she saw. Her eyes were intense as she stared, moving from one person to another.

"Okay, little girl," Mr. Paul said softly. "You've had enough." He led the foal away from Stormy. "Open that door for me, will you?" he asked.

Mandy unlatched the door and swung it wide.

"It's plain to see that Stormy doesn't want her little girl," he said sadly. "So we'll just put her in the next stall down. She'll be able to see her momma but Stormy won't be able to hurt her."

Hurt her? Could Stormy hurt her own baby? "Would she do that?" Tiffany asked.

"I don't know," Mr. Paul said. "But I'm not taking any chances. She sure isn't thrilled about this one." He rubbed the filly's nose, then lifted her in his arms and carried her out into the aisleway.

"Would you girls get that empty stall ready for her?" he asked.

Already Mandy was dragging a bale of straw down the aisle and into the stall. She cut it open with the shears and Tiffany jumped in, grabbed some straw, and scattered it on the dry floor. She and Mandy used the whole bale, making it extra deep. The little filly would need to stay warm and feel safe. She had no mother to snuggle up against, no warm touch to settle her. The straw would have to be soft and comforting.

Carefully, Mr. Paul carried the newborn into the stall. He put her down in the straw. It came up to her knees. The pinto reached down and touched it with her nose, rooting for a moment. Then her knees buckled and she sank into the bedding, stretching out and resting her head in it. As she closed her eyes, Mr. Paul shooed them from the stall and closed the door. "Let her rest," he said.

"Will she be okay?" Tiffany asked again.

"Don't know." His answer was quick and short, but then he looked down at Tiffany and his hand fell to her shoulder. "Honestly, it doesn't look good, Tiffany," he said. "Stormy doesn't want this one. I could make her nurse it tonight, but she's still weak from giving birth. When she gets stronger, she might not let me do that. She might not ever let that little filly nurse again."

Tiffany dropped back behind Mom and Mr. Paul. Falling into step with Mandy, their eyes locked and she could see the same worry reflected in Mandy's eyes that she felt inside.

Late that night, Tiffany lay in her bed as still as the night itself. It was hot and sticky and humid and Tiffany felt the same way inside. All clogged up. *How could a mother reject her own baby?* Then a chilling thought came over her. The same thing had happened to her.

eight

The next day Tiffany walked the road to the pony farm alone. The day was as humid as the night had been, and the sun shone through a fuzzy haze. She stomped at the tar bubbles rising in the road and thought about the foal. Poor little thing, all alone in a big new world. *She* was lucky, Tiffany decided about herself. Even if the woman who gave birth to her hadn't wanted her, she had a real mother waiting to take her. Stormy's filly was all alone.

Mandy was already at the farm when Tiffany arrived. It seemed as if she was always there. She was hanging over the stall door, watching the filly. It was standing in a corner of the stall, looking lost in a sea of yellow straw.

"How is she?" Tiffany asked.

"Stormy wouldn't let her nurse," Mandy said. "Mr. Paul tried some formula, but she didn't get much. Most of it just ran out of her mouth and she wouldn't swallow it."

Tiffany saw a can as big as a paint can sitting by the stall. It said Foal-Lac on its side. "That?" she asked.

"Yea," Mandy answered. "It's a powder. Mr. Paul mixed it with warm water and gave it to her in a bottle. She didn't like it though."

Tiffany remembered having once tasted powdered milk. "I don't blame her," she said. "Powder mixed with water . . . yuck!" She looked at the filly again.

Her head was hanging, almost to her knees. She looked so dejected.

Tiffany opened the stall door and slipped inside. She dropped beside the tiny pinto. The baby lifted her head and rested it on Tiffany's shoulder, whuffing warm breaths into Tiffany's ear. She wrapped her arms around the newborn and buried her head in her fuzzy coat. "You poor thing," she whispered again.

"I feel the same way," Mandy said softly. "Mr. Paul said this one is almost marked like Misty, her grandmother. She's not the same color as Misty, but she still looks like her in many ways. He might name the filly Misty II," Mandy added.

"Misty II," Tiffany whispered softly. It seemed to fit the tiny filly. She was soft and fuzzy-looking, like mist.

All at once, Mr. Paul came barreling down the aisle. "Girls! Come quick," he shouted. "Windy's down. She's going to foal at any minute!"

Tiffany jumped up, patting the filly. Then she hurried out of the stall. Mandy sprinted from the barn behind Mr. Paul and Tiffany followed. She saw Windy on the other side of the pasture, on her side, lying under the big maple tree. Her breath caught in her throat at the sight of her favorite mare lying down. "Please," she whispered. "Let everything go okay. Let Windy and the foal be alright." Her thoughts finished her wish. *And make Windy want her foal. Make her love it.*

Mr. Paul had some soft rags, a bucket of warm water and a bottle of iodine. He knelt down beside Windy's head. "You're alright," he said. "We'll take good care of you."

Mandy stood behind Mr. Paul and Tiffany knelt behind Windy's neck. She smoothed the strands of long mane in her hand. "Good girl," she said quietly. Then she leaned to whisper in Windy's ear. "I'm here now," she said. Windy rolled her eyes to look up at Tiffany, as if she knew it was okay now. Then she snorted.

Tiffany watched as the mare's stomach tightened

again and again. It wasn't long until the foal slid from her, front hooves first, followed by the head with a little muzzle almost resting on the front hooves. Then came the shoulders, and all of it wrapped in a shroud. Like the sheer white curtains that hung from Tiffany's bedroom windows, a transparent veil covered the newborn.

Tiffany held her breath and watched as the foal broke the shroud with a front hoof and a muzzle.

Windy turned to look at her new foal curiously. Then it seemed like only a few minutes before Windy struggled to stand, tearing the shroud. Tiffany and Mandy each followed Mr. Paul's lead, moving back quietly and watching.

Windy lowered her nose to the ground and nosed her newborn foal softly. She snorted, pushing away the remainder of the sac. She licked her foal's face with a long swipe of her tongue. Then another and another. The little one's eyes were already open and it gazed at its mother trance-like.

"It's a boy!" Mr. Paul said softly as the colt began to thrash his legs like a windmill. "He's like a little cyclone!"

A moment later the colt was struggling to stand.

Tiffany gasped. "He's already trying to stand up. Is that okay?" She looked to Mr. Paul.

Mr. Paul's face was split with a grin and he was nodding and rubbing his spiky hair. "You bet it is. This is how a foaling is supposed to go!"

Windy licked and nosed her new son, urging him along. He would get halfway up, stumble forward, then fall to the ground again. Sometimes he went backward, his legs pedaling for all their worth, seeking balance, then losing it and crumbling to the ground again. Each time he tried to stand he fell, but he didn't give up.

Tiffany and Mandy watched side by side while Mr. Paul leaned against the trunk of the maple. Tiffany was surprised when she felt Mandy's hand grasp her own. She looked at her new friend and grinned.

She felt like she was struggling with the colt and

falling with him. She wished and willed for him to make it to his feet, and soon the colt *was* standing, wobbling unsteadily beside his momma. Windy nuzzled him gently, pushing him toward the milk, and then he was nursing, sucking in great gulps, his eyes closed contentedly, his whole body rocking with the motion of his sucking.

Tiffany felt tears well in her eyes. First, watching the birth and now this . . . it was more wonderful than anything she had ever seen. She looked at Mr. Paul and Mandy. Mandy's eyes were as full as her own, threatening to spill tears of joy. Mr. Paul was rubbing his hair again, all smiles and sparkle.

"Guess I don't need this," he said, indicating the bucket and rags. "She's cleaning him off on her own."

Sure enough, Windy was scrubbing the newborn clean with her long, rough tongue. Lovingly and gently she introduced herself to her son.

"And God took a handful of southerly wind, blew his breath over it and created the horse," Mr. Paul said.

"What's that?" Mandy asked.

"It's a Bedouin legend," he said. "I think of it every time I see a foal come into the world."

Tiffany watched the tiny foal, another brown and white pinto. This one had a lot more white on its sides than Stormy's filly and his back was completely white. But the triangle of white on the left side of his neck just under the top of the mane was just the same, and so was the wide white blaze that ran down his face. The wind ruffled the scrubby fluff of mane along his neck and Mandy could see where the Bedouin legend might have come from. The colt was so beautiful, like the wind and everything natural. Only God's breath could have created something so perfect.

Mr. Paul moved forward and Windy lowered her nose to be scratched. She rolled her eyes toward the colt, then back at Mr. Paul. She seemed proud of her new son and both girls giggled at her antics.

Mr. Paul used a swab to brush some iodine on the underbelly of the new foal. "It keeps infection out," he explained at Tiffany's puzzled look. "Come on, girls," he said, gathering up the bucket and rags. "It's time to leave these two to themselves. We've got barn chores to do."

Reluctantly, Tiffany followed Mr. Paul and Mandy from the field. She watched Windy one more time before leaving. The mare was licking the colt's neck and the colt was nursing by her side.

Later that day, Tiffany followed Mr. Paul back to the pasture. The stalls were clean and the feed bins filled. There was fresh hay in each stall along with clean buckets of water. Before Mandy's mom had picked her up to go home the girls had prepared a stall for Windy and her new colt next to Stormy's filly. "If she can see the new colt, maybe she'll feel less alone," Mandy had said, and Mr. Paul had agreed.

Windy came to them as soon as they entered the pasture. The newborn trotted alongside her. "Look at him go," Tiffany said. "You sure were right when you said he was like a cyclone," she said, seeing the power in his legs as they carried him by his mother's side.

"By golly," Mr. Paul said as he clipped a lead shank to Windy and led her inside. "I believe that's a perfect name for this little one. We'll call him Cyclone."

Tiffany laughed. Cyclone followed Windy into the stall. Stormy's frail filly watched through the wooden rails with a look of curiosity. She stumbled forward, shoving her nose over the rail. Then a weak, high pitched squeal rang out. It was the first sound the filly had ever made other than sniffing and sucking. Windy's head shot up at the sound. She peered over the rail at the filly, her own colt sidestepping tight against her.

Tiffany saw Windy's big brown eyes roll toward the filly and she felt hope spring up inside of her. "She likes the filly," she half whispered, half spoke.

Mr. Paul smiled and nodded. "She might just take this one."

"What do you mean?" Tiffany asked.

"She might be willing to adopt the filly, too.

Sometimes a mare will take care of another mare's foal. Sometimes they won't. But, the good ones will do it."

Tiffany felt tears spring to her eyes for the second time that day and hope filled her. The filly would have a chance now, because Windy was definitely one of the good ones. Tiffany knew it as well as she knew Windy herself. The filly would finally have a chance at life.

nine

"Wake up, Tiffany," Mom whispered. "Get up." Tiffany's eyes flew wide. "What? What is it? Mom?" she asked. She sat up in bed, rubbing her eyes. The sun cast a grey pall into the room. Her alarm clock read 6 A.M.

"Mr. Paul called. He wants to know if you can come."

Tiffany scrambled from the bed, throwing off her nightgown and pulling open dresser drawers as she spoke. "What's wrong? Is it Windy? Why does he want me this early?"

"Calm down, honey," Mom said. "Mr. Paul said the filly is weak. He wants to try her with Windy, but he wants you there, first. He said you have a way with Windy. He said you calm her . . . that you two share a bond."

Despite her worry, what Mom said warmed her. She knew she shared a bond with Windy, but she didn't know anyone else had noticed. She pulled jeans from her bottom drawer and a t-shirt from another. Mom shut the drawers behind her daughter and smoothed her hair after the t-shirt was on.

Tiffany hurried to wash her face and brush her hair while Mom hovered nearby. "Do you want to go?" she asked her mom through a mouthful of foaming toothpaste.

"Sure. I'd like that," Mom said. "I'll drive us over so you can get there quicker."

They found Mr. Paul in little Misty II's stall. He had the rag again, scrubbing the foal's neck and legs softly. She wasn't wet, but she needed the love and attention. Tiffany knew that. Windy was pacing in her stall next door, her colt curled up in a corner, sleeping soundly. She rubbed her muzzle over the bars that separated the filly from her, watching.

"She took a little more Foal-Lac last night and a little this morning," Mr. Paul said of Misty II. "But it just isn't enough to keep her going. Stormy won't even let her near. But Windy's been carrying on, mooing like a cow at her all morning."

At the mention of her name, Windy rubbed her muzzle over the bars again, and a soft moaning moo escaped her lips. It wasn't the whinny or the neigh that Tiffany was accustomed to hearing. It *did* sound like a cow's moo! But it was soft and gentle and full of concern.

"See what I mean?" Mr. Paul said. "I thought as long as she was acting like that we ought to try putting these two together."

Tiffany nodded and reached for Windy. Windy leaned over the stall door and burrowed her head in Tiffany's shirt. "There, there," Tiffany said softly. "Are you worried about that little one?"

Windy's head rose and she searched Tiffany's face as if she needed an answer to some unasked question. Then she went back to pacing and stopping to stare through the bars at Misty II.

"Do you want to lead her in with Misty II?" Mr. Paul asked. "I'll help the filly up if you think you can handle Windy."

"Sure I can. She's my buddy. Aren't you girl?" she asked the mare, and Windy pressed her head into Tiffany's jacket in reply. Tiffany reached up to unclip the lead shank that hung by the door. She hooked it onto Windy's halter. While Mom held the door open wide, she led the mare out and into the next stall.

Mr. Paul held Misty II up. "Before we try this I better tell you a few things," he said. "Windy might not be as thrilled about this as we all hope she'll be. If she starts to nip or kick or anything crazy, you just get her out of here and let me worry about the filly. Okay?"

Tiffany nodded. She couldn't imagine Windy doing anything like that, but she would be careful just the same.

Slowly, Mr. Paul brought the filly to meet Windy. Windy's eyes had not left the filly's face, and now she snorted her pleasure and stretched her neck to meet the little pinto. All of Tiffany's worries were cast aside when Windy began to wash the white blaze that ran down the tiny face. The mare's tongue was so big and rough that Misty II would have been knocked off of her feet had Mr. Paul not been there to help. Windy nosed Misty II, shoving her tiny body back and toward the milk.

It was only a moment until the filly was nursing. Windy stood as still as a statue, watching the new-born for a few moments. Then she resumed licking and scrubbing, absorbing the scents of her new daughter, fulfilling a pony promise.

Tiffany felt Mom's arm come around her as they watched it all. Noisily, Misty II rooted and suckled with all of her might. Her tail switched from side to side and her whole body swayed with the motion of it all. Mr. Paul unclipped the lead shank from Windy's halter and the three of them filed from the stall.

"She's a good one," Mr. Paul said.

"Looks like she's got a new baby daughter," Mom added, and her arm gripped Tiffany's shoulder even more tightly.

As they watched the mare and the filly, Tiffany's thoughts turned to her mom. Windy was a lot like her own mom, Tiffany thought. She was strong and loving. She was quiet when Tiffany needed someone to listen, and she was there when Tiffany needed someone to hug. That is what a *real* mother is all about, Tiffany thought.

It's not who gives birth to you, but who is there when you are sick and in need, like the filly. It's not who gives birth to you, but who really cares.

Suddenly Tiffany realized that she *was* a Clark after all. She was a Clark in the most important way. She belonged.

As she watched Windy nurse the little filly, Tiffany realized that, even in nature, there are real mothers, and mothers who can't always care for their young. Even animals adopt, Tiffany thought, and it surprised her.

Wrapping her arms around her mom's waist, Tiffany hugged her tight.

A moment later Cyclone was awake and nickering for his momma. Mr. Paul led the little colt next door to meet his new sister. The filly had finished nursing and looked up expectantly at the colt as he charged inside. Windy lowered her head to greet her son, then took turns licking each one. She rumbled with satisfaction as she watched her new family. Tiffany smiled, feeling the same satisfaction deep inside.

AUTHOR'S NOTE

While this story is fictionalized, the characters of Misty, Stormy, Windy, Cyclone, and Misty II are based on real Chincoteague ponies. Windy did give birth to a colt named Cyclone at about the same time her mother Stormy gave birth to the filly, Misty II. Stormy rejected her new foal, although there is some debate about whether it was at birth, or shortly thereafter. Windy adopted Stormy's foal and raised it alongside of her own.

Today Windy and Cyclone reside in Waynesboro, Pennsylvania. Windy is the oldest living Misty descendant. Misty II lives in Manheim, Pennsylvania, and has become a successful show pony. Stormy died peacefully on a farm in Waynesboro, Pennsylvania just before Thanksgiving of 1993. She was thirty-one years old.

Paul Merritt still owns and operates the Misty Museum on Chincoteague Island in Virginia, where this story takes place.

For more charming ponies
and a collectible pony charm don't miss:

CHARMING PONIES

A Perfect Pony

Will Niki choose the pony of her dreams?

Turn the page for a sneak peek!

one

Niki Crawford jumped out of the pickup truck almost before it had even stopped. Horses and riders milled about on the edge of the parking lot, and a long, blue horse trailer was backing up to a ramp that led into the stockyard. Floodlights lit the whole area, including the white letters on the side of the building that read LIVESTOCK AUCTION.

"Wait up, Niki!" Dad puffed as he slid out of the driver's seat. "Those horses aren't going anywhere without you."

Niki turned and grinned at her dad, her dark eyes twinkling. He was older than most of her friends' fathers, but the thinning gray hair and the slight limp didn't bother Niki. He was still "good ol' Dad." They had been on their own for as long as Niki could remember. Her mother had died when Niki was young.

Slowing her step, she waited for her father. She felt for the lump of rolled money in her back pocket, running her hand over it to make sure it was still there. A ripple of nervous jitters ran through her. *Tonight's the night*, she thought. *I'm finally going to get my own horse.*

Dad put a hand on Niki's long dark hair, and they walked inside together. "Nervous?" he asked, and she nodded.

"I can't believe it's finally happening," she said out loud.

"You earned it," Dad answered matter-of-factly. "That was the deal. You earn it. You pay for it. You take care of it." He paused. "The hard part's ahead of you."

Niki frowned as she looked into her Dad's blue eyes. "You know I'll take care of it. I've wanted a horse for so long . . ." her voice trailed off; then she added softly, "I can't wait to take care of it."

Inside the auction barn Dad stopped to talk to old friends, and Niki wandered down the aisles. They had come here every Saturday night since Niki was little. Dad came to visit with friends from neighboring farms. Niki came for the horses.

Inside the ring, she heard the auctioneer beginning to sell the tack. She knew they would sell the saddles and bridles, brushes and tools for at least another hour before the horses and ponies were led in.

As Niki came to the first row of horses, she stopped to evaluate each one. She was looking for the perfect pony, the pony of her dreams. Would it be a chestnut or a bay, a pinto or a gray? It didn't matter to Niki what color it was. What mattered was something else. Maybe a certain look in its eye or the way it carried itself. Heck, she wasn't even quite sure what it would be. But she was sure that she would know it when she saw her special horse. She would just know.

In the first square pen was a tall, chestnut thoroughbred with two white stockings. He paced from side to side and threw back his head, his eyes rolling wildly. Sticking her head through the top two rails, Niki peered up at the chestnut. All at once he drew himself up and let out a loud whinny. Niki jumped so quick that she bumped her head on the top rail.

She rubbed her head as she moved on to the next pen. There she looked in at a tiny pinto mare with a young foal at its side. A crowd was already gathering around this pen, and Niki knew that the pair would bring a high price. She called it the "cute factor." Whenever there was a fuzzy or cute or young pony, the crowd would "ooh" and "ahh" and the animals would sell for a high price. She moved on.

Down the row she looked at a sturdy bay pony saddled in Western gear. He looked like a nice pony, but not special. She studied a dapple gray yearling for quite some time. It seemed sensitive enough, but it would be another year until she could ride it. There were two pintos—a tall, rangy looking sorrel and a stocky blood bay. Nothing special. Niki was beginning to get discouraged.

She'd worked so hard this summer, helping on the farm, earning the money the hard way, like Daddy said she had to, and now . . . where was her pony?

Turning back to the blue trailer, Niki watched as the driver and his partner returned from the business office to unload their cargo. The first one off was a magnificent black-and-white pinto with a flowing black tail. Niki felt her heart pound as she watched it come down the aisle, right past her and into a holding pen. But if she was impressed with the pinto, she was totally unprepared for the next one.

Her breath caught in her throat as she watched a pure white mare come off the trailer and down the ramp. The mane hung in long silvery strands and she held her head high. She was calm, Niki noticed. That was a trait she was looking for. But there was even more. A large pony, the mare was just the right height. She picked her hooves up daintily as she stepped through the dirty stockyard, almost as if it was not quite clean enough for her.

"Princess," Niki mumbled. The pony was an absolute princess. Then it came down the aisle right beside her, and Niki felt her heart explode as the mare tossed her head. By the time they had closed the gate of the holding pen, Niki was really excited. She reached back to feel the money in her pocket and she knew it would be enough. "Princess" was the one.

When the men had penned her and the vet had finished drawing blood from her neck for the required health check, Niki sidled closer. The man who had led the mare down the ramp and into the pen was a cowboy with a wide-brimmed hat. Now, as he left the pen, he slapped a sticker on the mare's rump: 56. Princess was number 56. It etched itself into

Niki's brain. The number she needed to bid on would be 56. The cowboy grinned at her. "She's a good one, little miss," he said, and Niki blushed. Was it so obvious that she was taken with the mare?

After the men had left, Niki clucked to the mare and she came right over. The face was long and dish-shaped, like an Arabian, with a tiny teacup nose and wide, deep-set eyes. They were soft and brown and they watched Niki closely as she reached through the rails to pat the horse on the shoulder. Without hesitation, the mare lowered her head and her velvety muzzle settled into Niki's hand. *With a spiraled horn she could be a unicorn from a fairy tale*, Niki thought.

There was a commotion behind her and a high-pitched whine rang out. "I want that one, Mamma! You gotta git me that one over there!"

A heavyset woman with rosy cheeks and a big stain on the front of her too tight T-shirt was coming down the aisle. With her hand clasped firmly in his, she was fairly dragging along a chubby little boy with a crew cut. But the whine had not come from the small child. It had come from nine-year-old Billy Baily. Niki knew him. He was in her class at school and he was a royal pain. Now he was pointing at her Princess.

Then he caught sight of Niki. "Hey! It's N*iiii*ki!" he crooned. "Icky, picky, sticky, Niki! Whatta you doin' here, Icky?"

Niki whirled around with her hands on her hips. "Same thing as you, Billy," she said. "It's a free country."

Instead of answering her Billy stuck his fingers in his ears and twirled them around, his tongue hanging out the side of his mouth and his eyes rolling up.

Niki turned and marched down the aisle, away from Billy and away from Princess. "Some people never grow up . . . Billy!" she said over her shoulder.

As Billy's whiney voice faded behind her, Niki hurried forward. There was a crowd gathered around another holding pen where a pony had just been unloaded. *Probably another "cute factor,"* she thought, but she knew she had to see for herself.

She heard the comment of a lady in front of her before she even saw the pony. "Poor, dear thing," the lady said under her breath.

After pushing her way through the sea of legs and bodies gathered around the rails, Niki knelt down and peered into the pen through the bottom rails. The pony was a little bit shorter than Princess, coal black with four white stockings and a narrow white blaze running down the length of his face. She could see his face clearly because it was hanging down to his knees, which were buckled from the sheer energy of holding himself up. Every rib protruded in agonizing detail and he heaved soft whuffing breaths. If it weren't for the way his spindley legs were braced, he would surely have been on the ground.

Niki's heart, which moments ago had danced with happiness, now dropped to her stomach. She fought a sick feeling that was oozing up from inside of her as she looked into the pony's glazed eyes.

"The doggers will buy this one for sure," she heard someone say and others grunted in agreement.

No! she thought angrily. How could they say that? How could they let the dog food buyers get him before he even had a chance? He had already suffered enough. Then, to die for that . . . to become canned dog food! It just wasn't fair.

Niki's hand snaked through the rails to stroke the pony's long white blaze. Slowly, the pony lifted his black head and met her gaze. He held her stare for a moment before dropping his head back down again. But that moment was all it took.

LOIS SZYMANSKI

is the author of many books for young readers. She lives in Westminster, Maryland, with her husband, two daughters, and three cats. She and her older daughter have four horses-one of them a Chincoteague pony named Sea Feather. When Lois isn't writing, she stays busy taking care of her family, talking to students in the classroom, and dreaming up new stories about horses.

YOU CAN VISIT LOIS ONLINE AT
www.angelfire.com/md/childauth/